PRO SPORTS SUPERSTARS

SUPERSTARS OF THE DALLAS COWBOYS

by M.K. Osborne

AMICUS | AMICUS INK

Amicus High Interest and Amicus Ink are imprints of Amicus
P.O. Box 1329, Mankato, MN 56002
www.amicuspublishing.us

Library of Congress Cataloging-in-Publication Data
Names: Osborne, M. K., author.
Title: Superstars of the Dallas Cowboys / By M.K. Osborne.
Description: Mankato, MN : Amicus, [2019] |
Series: Pro sports superstars NFL. | Includes index. | Audience: K to Grade 3.
Identifiers: LCCN 2017057273 (print) | LCCN 2018006976 (ebook) | ISBN 9781681514857 (pdf) | ISBN 9781681514031 (library binding) | ISBN 9781681523231 (pbk.)
Subjects: LCSH: Dallas Cowboys (Football team)--Biography--Juvenile literature. | Dallas Cowboys (Football team)--History--Juvenile literature. | Football players--United States--Biography--Juvenile literature.
Classification: LCC GV956.D3 (ebook) | LCC GV956.D3 O74 2019 (print) | DDC 796.332/64097642812--dc23
LC record available at https://lccn.loc.gov/2017057273

Photo Credits: AP Images/Associated Press, cover, 16–17, 18–19, 20–21; ESPN Images/ Scott Clarke, 4–5, 14–15; Getty Images/Focus On Sport, 6–7, 8–9, 12–13, George Rose/ Stringer, 10–11

Series Designer: Veronica Scott
Book Designer: Ciara Beitlich/ Veronica Scott
Photo Researcher: Holly Young

Printed in China
HC 10 9 8 7 6 5 4 3 2 1
PB 10 9 8 7 6 5 4 3 2 1

TABLE OF CONTENTS

GET TO KNOW THE COWBOYS

The Dallas Cowboys have been to eight Super Bowls. They won five of them. Most of their fans are in Texas. But they also have fans all over the United States.

Who are some of the Cowboys' greatest stars? Let's find out!

BOB LILLY

It took two men to block Bob Lilly. He played **defense**. Lilly went to 11 **Pro Bowls**. He helped the Cowboys win a Super Bowl in 1971. Lilly was the first Cowboy to be in the **NFL** Hall of Fame.

ROGER STAUBACH

Roger Staubach was a great **quarterback**. He was known for making big plays. He went to four Super Bowls. The Cowboys won two of them, in 1972 and 1978.

Staubach was named **MVP** of the 1972 Super Bowl.

TONY DORSETT

Tony Dorsett was a good runner. It was hard for tacklers to catch him. He was the **Rookie** of the Year in 1977. Dorsett ran 99 yards for a touchdown in 1982. That is still the longest run of all time in the NFL.

EMMITT SMITH

Emmitt Smith was a **running back**. The Cowboys picked him in the first round of the 1990 **draft**. Smith helped the Cowboys win three Super Bowls. In 1994, he was named the Super Bowl MVP.

Smith led the NFL with 113 catches in 2001.

TONY ROMO

Tony Romo was a smart quarterback. He was fast. He could throw the ball well. He went to four Pro Bowls. He played with the Cowboys for 14 years. He retired in 2017.

JASON WITTEN

Jason Witten was drafted for the Cowboys in 2003. He is one of the best tight ends in the NFL. In 2012 he caught 110 passes. Witten holds the team record for receptions.

Witten has played in 10 Pro Bowls.

50

SEAN LEE

Sean Lee has played for the Cowboys since 2010. He is a record-setting linebacker. He is a star defensive player and excels at tackling. Lee made 174 tackles in 2016.

YOUNG STAR

Dak Prescott was an underdog at first. But now fans love him. He had 13 wins as a rookie quarterback in 2016. He also had six rushing touchdowns in one season. That is a Cowboys record for quarterbacks.

Let's watch and see who will be the next star of the Cowboys!

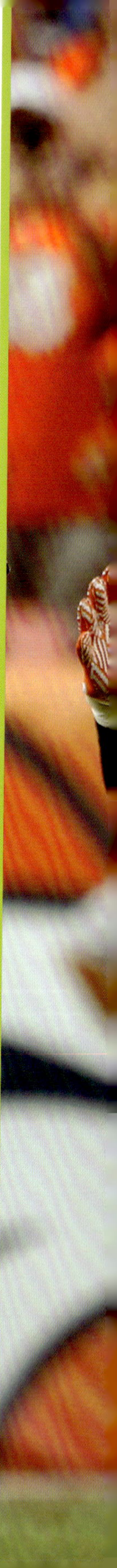

Prescott played in a Pro Bowl as a rookie.

TEAM FAST FACTS

Founded: 1960

Home Stadium: AT&T Stadium
(Arlington, Texas)

Super Bowl Titles: 5
(1972, 1978, 1993, 1994 and 1996)

Nicknames: America's Team, The Boys

Hall of Fame Players: 20
including Bob Lilly, Roger Staubach, Tony Dorsett, and Emmitt Smith

WORDS TO KNOW

defense – the group of players that tries to stop the other team from scoring

draft – an event where teams choose new players from college football teams

MVP – Most Valuable Player; an honor given to the best player each season

NFL – National Football League; a group that organizes and promotes pro football games

Pro Bowl – the NFL's all-star game

quarterback – a player whose main jobs are to lead the offense and throw passes

rookie – a player in his first season

running back – a player whose main job is running with the ball

LEARN MORE

Books

Frisch, Aaron. *Dallas Cowboys*. Mankato, Minn: Creative Education, 2014.

Mack, Larry. *The Dallas Cowboys Story*. Minneapolis: Bellwether Media, 2017.

Websites

Dallas Cowboys—Official Site
http://www.dallascowboys.com
Watch video clips and view photos of the Dallas Cowboys.

NFL.com
http://nfl.com
Check out pictures and your favorite football players' stats.

NFL Rush
http://www.nflrush.com
Play games and learn how to be a part of NFL PLAY 60.

INDEX